Madison
and the
New Neighbors

By
Vanita Braver

Illustrated by
Jonathan Brown

Published in the United States of America by Star Bright Books, Inc.
The name Star Bright Books and the Star Bright Books logo are registered trademarks of Star Bright Books, Inc. Please visit: www.starbrightbooks.com. For bulk orders, email: orders@starbrightbooks.com, or call customer service at: (617) 354-1300.

Hardback ISBN-13: 978-1-59572-686-5
Star Bright Books / MA/ 00110140
Paperback ISBN-13: 978-1-59572-687-2
Star Bright Books / MA / 00110140

Printed in China (WKT) 10 9 8 7 6 5 4 3 2 1

Printed on paper from sustainable forests and a percentage of post-consumer paper.

Library of Congress Cataloging-in-Publication Data

Braver, Vanita.
 Madison and the new neighbors / by Dr. Vanita Braver ; illustrated by Jonathan Brown.
    pages cm. – (Teach your children well)
 Summary: When Madison's mother takes her through the neighborhood to sell candy for school, Madison refuses to go to one particular house because the girl who moved there from India has a strange accent, but after being reminded of how she felt when she first moved, Madison gives Seema a chance.
  ISBN 978-1-59572-686-5 (hardcover : alk. paper) – ISBN 978-1-59572-687-2 (pbk. : alk. paper)
 [1. Moving, Household–Fiction. 2. Neighborliness–Fiction. 3. East Indian Americans–Fiction. 4. Fund raising–Fiction.] I. Brown, Jonathan, 1963- illustrator. II. Title.
 PZ7.B73795Mag 2014
 [E]--dc23
                            2014015093

To Ellen DeGeneres,
Thank you for teaching us about tolerance and respecting
differences. Your generous spirit reminds us that life's challenges,
obstacles, and the choices we make define who we are. — V.B.

To Julia and Violet, who open my eyes. — J.B.

Madison ran to her mom as soon as she stepped off the school bus.

"Mommy, guess what? I have to sell candy to raise money for my class. If I sell enough, I get a school T-shirt. Will you help me?" she asked.

"Sure, honey. After you've done your homework, we can visit some of the neighbors and see if they would be interested," said her mom.

When Madison finished her homework, she and her mom walked next door to Mrs. Phillips's house.

"Hi! Madison, you've gotten so tall!"

"Hi, Mrs. Phillips. I'm selling candy to raise money for my class. Would you like to buy some?" inquired Madison.

"Let's see what you've got," said Mrs. Phillips as she looked through the brochure. "I'll take a box of these assorted chocolates and a box of these with the nuts. I'm sure they will be delicious!"

"Thank you," said Madison with a smile. Mrs. Phillips smiled back and filled out the order form.

They said goodbye and Madison and her mom walked toward the next house.

"Can we skip this house?" asked Madison.

"Why, Madison?"

"Seema Patel lives there."

"Do you know her?" asked her mom.

"Yes. She talks with a funny accent. No one sits next to her on the bus," said Madison.

"Madison, that's not nice. They just moved here from India," said her mom. "I've met Mrs. Patel. She's nice. We should get to know them."

"But, Mom, everyone on the bus makes fun of Seema. They think she's weird," replied Madison.

"Madison, you know that's not kind. Seema has an accent because she is from another country. People from different countries have different accents and customs that are unique to them. It's fun to learn about them," explained her mom.

"I don't care. I don't want to go there," declared Madison.

"I bet Seema feels lonely. Imagine what you would feel like if we moved to another country? Now, let's go," Madison's mom said, reaching for her hand.

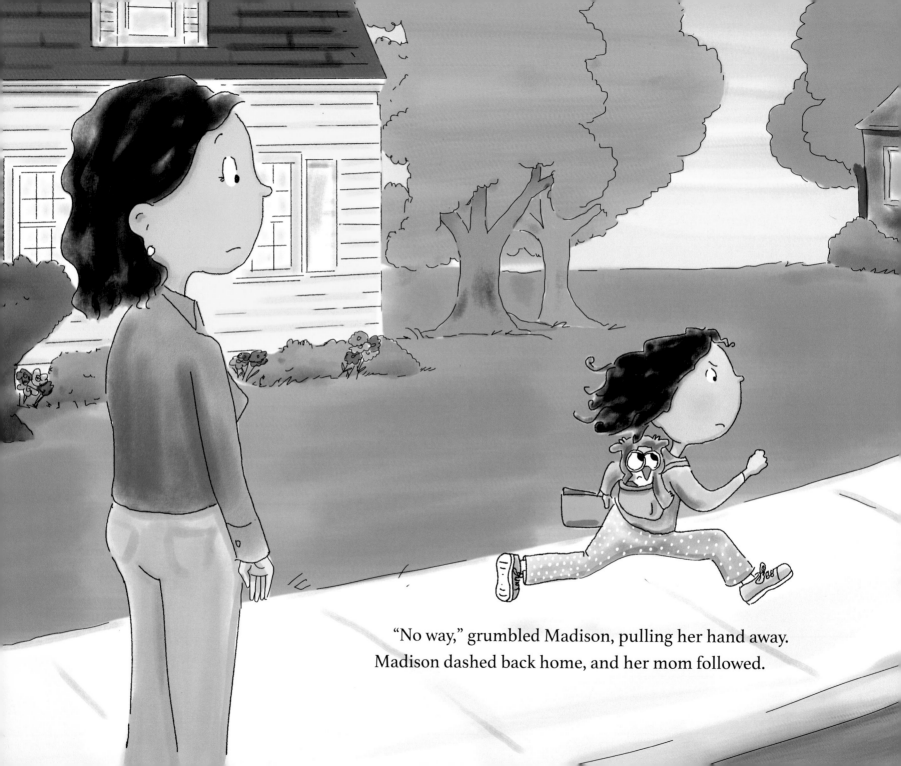

"No way," grumbled Madison, pulling her hand away.
Madison dashed back home, and her mom followed.

Once inside, Madison turned on the television and sat on the couch. Her mom turned off the television and said, "Madison, you know better than to run off like that. I think we should go to Seema's house. Think about it. In the meantime, I'm going to get dinner started."

Madison stomped upstairs to her room.

Her dad opened the door and said, "Madison, I heard you slam the door. That's not acceptable behavior."

"Dad, I don't want to go to Seema's house. She's different. She's from India. Mom thinks I should be friends with her."

"It's up to you, Sweetie. Do you remember how you felt when we first moved here? We weren't even from another country." Madison's dad then gently tossed her stuffed owl Wisdom to her as he left the room.

Madison caught Wisdom and went to her table to play with her jigsaw puzzle, but she had trouble getting the pieces to fit. She just could not pay attention. She was thinking about Seema. She thought about how she would feel if she was in a new country. "I felt lonely when I was new at school and no one sat next to me. Seema has it worse. At least the kids didn't tease me." She hugged Wisdom.

Madison went downstairs. Her mom was in the kitchen slicing carrots and cucumbers. Madison walked in and said, "I guess we can go to the Patels'."

"Fine, but we should go before it gets too late," answered her mom.

"Okay," Madison said, grabbing a cucumber slice.

Madison and her mom walked to the Patels' house and rang the doorbell.

Mrs. Patel opened the door. She was wearing a beautiful blue sari.

"Hi," said Madison's mom. "We've been meaning to come by. This is my daughter, Madison."

"Nice to meet you Madison. I've seen you at the bus stop," said Mrs. Patel.

"Hi," said Madison. "I'm selling candy to raise money for my class."

"Seema is also selling candy. I'll buy some from both of you."

"And I'll buy some from Seema," said Madison's mom. "Is she home?"

"Yes, come on in. She's in the family room," said Seema's mom.

Inside, Madison and her mom smelled the wonderful aroma of spices and admired the beautiful pieces from India. There was an elaborate bronze vase with peacock feathers and a wooden coffee table with an intricate elephant design carved into it.

"Hi," said Madison.

"Hi," responded Seema.

"Our moms are going to buy candy from both of us. They are trying to decide what to buy," explained Madison.

"I like your owl," said Seema. "I've just unpacked my doll collection. Do you want to see it?"

They both went upstairs. Madison's eyes lit up. She could not believe how beautiful Seema's dolls were. Seema collected dolls from all over the world.

"Wow! Look at the beautiful dress on this doll. I love her," said Madison.

"Oh, that's Lin. She is from China, but this one is my favorite," said Seema as she pointed to a doll wearing a pink sari. "I call her Pritti. It means pretty. She is from India, like me."

"Oh, she's so beautiful," replied Madison.

They played and talked, and then it was time to go.

Madison asked, "Do we have to go home so soon?"
Seema added, "Can Madison stay a little longer?"
"Well, just a little while," replied Madison's mom.

When Madison and her mom were leaving, Mrs. Patel handed them a bowl of food.

"Madison, this is Vegetable Biryani for you. It is made with vegetables, rice and spices," said Mrs. Patel.

"Oh, Vegetable Biryani," said Madison's mom. "Thank you. I would love the recipe."

"I love Biryani! " exclaimed Seema.

"I guess I will try it," replied Madison.

"See you on the bus tomorrow, Seema!" said Madison.

All the way home, Madison couldn't stop talking about Seema and her doll collection.

That night, when Madison's mom was tucking her in bed, she said,
"You and Seema got along well. I'm really pleased."

"Maybe Seema can come bike riding with Emily and me tomorrow,"
said Madison. "I like her even though she talks with an accent."

"I think she likes you too," replied her mom.

"I'm going to sit next to her on the school bus," said Madison.

Madison's mom smiled. "Now have a good night. I love you," she said.

"Good night, Mommy. I love you too," Madison replied as she gave her
mom a kiss good night.

Madison's mom left the room. Madison closed her eyes and all was quiet. Wisdom the Owl cuddled next to her.

As Madison was falling asleep, Wisdom whispered into her ear, "You should feel good about yourself—because you recognize that it's important to respect differences."

With that, Madison fell sound asleep.

Parent's Note

Dear Parent or Educator,

As a mom of three, an educator, and a practicing child and adolescent psychiatrist, I know that parenting is challenging at best: I have often said that I was the perfect parent until I had children!

I want what we all want for our children—to have them lead happy, enriching, and successful lives. But no matter who we are, the essence of being human is to undergo a wide range of experiences, both good and bad. Life presents us all with moral dilemmas, discrepancies of the heart and mind. How we live our lives and cope with difficult circumstances is a reflection of who we are and the choices we make.

One of life's greatest gifts is the ability to reflect, to ask questions of each other and of ourselves. Through this process, we learn to make good choices—and it's a gift that must be nurtured and learned. The *Teach Your Children Well* series models the dialogue and interactions that facilitate the critical thinking and self-reflection necessary for kids to learn to make moral, ethical choices.

We can make a difference in the world through the way we, as individuals, conduct our lives. Our children are really our greatest resource!

Warmly,
Dr. Vanita Braver

Ten Tips for Raising Moral Children:

1. Make raising moral children a priority. If you really want to raise moral children, then commit to it and put forth the effort.
2. Live by setting a moral example. Research has shown that parents are the most significant and powerful influence in their children's moral development.
3. Be clear about what you value, and communicate that. You can't adequately instill a belief in your children if it's not clear within you.
4. Set clear, reasonable, and challenging guidelines about what you expect from your children. Reinforce these at every opportunity, but be open to discussion.
5. Set clear boundaries and enforce limits. Understand that all children will test limits, and be consistent in your responses.
6. Recognize opportunities to teach. The most powerful and persuasive moral teaching opportunities present themselves in ordinary moments.
7. Emphasize the Golden Rule. Encourage your children to treat others the way they wish to be treated.
8. Reflection is a powerful, effective tool to stimulate internal motivation. Encourage your children to think through the consequences of their actions and their effects on others.
9. Reinforce positive behaviors. When your children make good choices, notice their behavior and express to them how it made you feel.
10. Listen actively and allow your children to think through dilemmas. Ask them questions that allow them to draw conclusions.